ish

Peter H. Reynolds

CANDLEWICK PRESS
CAMBRIDGE, MASSACHUSETTS

Ramon loved to draw.

Anytime.

Anything.

Anywhere.

One day, Ramon was drawing
a vase of flowers.
His brother, Leon,
leaned over his shoulder.

Leon burst out laughing.
"WHAT is THAT?" he asked.

Ramon could not even answer.
He just crumpled up the drawing
and threw it across the room.

Leon's laughter haunted Ramon.
He kept trying to make his
drawings look "right,"
but they never did.

After many months and
many crumpled sheets of paper,
Ramon put his pencil down.

"I'm done."

Marisol, his sister, was watching him.
"What do YOU want?" he snapped.

"I was watching you draw," she said.

Ramon sneered.
"I'm NOT drawing! Go away!"

Marisol ran away, but not before
picking up a crumpled sheet of paper.

"Hey! Come back here with that!"

Ramon raced after Marisol,
up the hall and into her room.

He was about to yell
but fell silent when
he saw his sister's walls....
He stared at the Crumpled gallery.

"This is one of my favorites,"
Marisol said, pointing.

"That was SUPPOSED to be a
vase of flowers," Ramon said,
"but it doesn't look like one."

"Well, it looks vase-ISH!"
she exclaimed.

"Vase-ISH?"

Ramon looked closer.
Then he studied all the drawings on
Marisol's walls and began to
see them in a whole new way.

"They do look . . . ish", he said.

Ramon felt light and energized.
Thinking ish-ly allowed
his ideas to flow freely.

He began to draw what he felt —
loose lines.
Quickly springing out.
Without worry.

Ramon once again drew
and drew the world around him.
Making an ish drawing
felt wonderful.

He filled his journals...

tree-ish

house-ish

boat-ish

afternoon-ish

fish-ish

sun-ish

Ramon realized he could draw ish feelings too.

peace-ish

silly-ish

excited-ish.

His ish art inspired ish writing.
He wasn't sure if he was writing poems,
but he knew they were poem-ish.

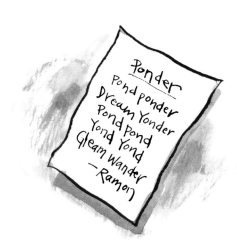

Ponder
Pond ponder
Dream Yonder
Pond Pond
Yond Yond
Gleam Wander
—Ramon

One spring morning,
Ramon had a wonderful feeling.
It was a feeling that even ish words
and ish drawings could not capture.
He decided NOT to capture it.
Instead, he simply savored it....

And Ramon lived ishfully ever after.

The End-ish

Dedicated to Doug Kornfeld, my art teacher, who
dared me to draw for myself and find my voice

First edition 2004

Library of Congress Cataloging-in-Publication Data is available.

Library of Congress Catalog Card Number 2003066196

ISBN 0-7636-2344-X

2 4 6 8 10 9 7 5 3 1

Printed in China

This book was hand lettered by Peter H. Reynolds.
The illustrations were done in watercolor, ink, and tea.

Candlewick Press
2067 Massachusetts Avenue
Cambridge, Massachusetts 02140

visit us at www.candlewick.com